Dear Parent:
Your child's love of reading

Every child learns to read in a different way and at his own speed. Some go back and forth between reading levels and read favorite books again and again. Others read through each level in order. You can help your young reader improve and become more confident by encouraging his or her own interests and abilities. From books your child reads with you to the first books he or she reads alone, there are I Can Read Books for every stage of reading:

SHARED READING
Basic language, word repetition, and whimsical illustrations, ideal for sharing with your emergent reader

BEGINNING READING
Short sentences, familiar words, and simple concepts for children eager to read on their own

READING WITH HELP
Engaging stories, longer sentences, and language play for developing readers

READING ALONE
Complex plots, challenging vocabulary, and high-interest topics for the independent reader

ADVANCED READING
Short paragraphs, chapters, and exciting themes for the perfect bridge to chapter books

I Can Read Books have introduced children to the joy of reading since 1957. Featuring award-winning authors and illustrators and a fabulous cast of beloved characters, I Can Read Books set the standard for beginning readers.

A lifetime of discovery begins with the magical words **"I Can Read!"**

*Visit www.icanread.com for information
on enriching your child's reading experience.*

I Can Read!

READING
2
WITH HELP

MEET THE X-MEN

Adapted by Harry Lime
Illustrated by Steven E. Gordon
Based on the motion picture screenplay
written by Simon Kinberg & Zak Penn

HarperCollins*Publishers*

HarperCollins®, ☁®, and I Can Read Book® are trademarks of HarperCollins Publishers.

X-Men: The Last Stand: Meet the X-Men
Marvel, X-Men and all related character names and the distinctive likenesses thereof are trademarks of Marvel Characters, Inc.
and are used with permission. Copyright © 2006 Marvel Characters, Inc. All rights reserved.
www.marvel.com
© 2006 Twentieth Century Fox Film Corporation
Printed in the United States of America.
No part of this book may be used or reproduced in any manner whatsoever without written permission
except in the case of brief quotations embodied in critical articles and reviews.
For information address HarperCollins Children's Books, a division of HarperCollins Publishers,
1350 Avenue of the Americas, New York, NY 10019.
www.icanread.com
Library of Congress catalog card number: 2006920162
ISBN-10: 0-06-082204-X—ISBN-13: 978-0-06-082204-0

1 2 3 4 5 6 7 8 9 10
❖
First Edition

Welcome to the School for Gifted Youngsters. Some of the students call it Mutant High.

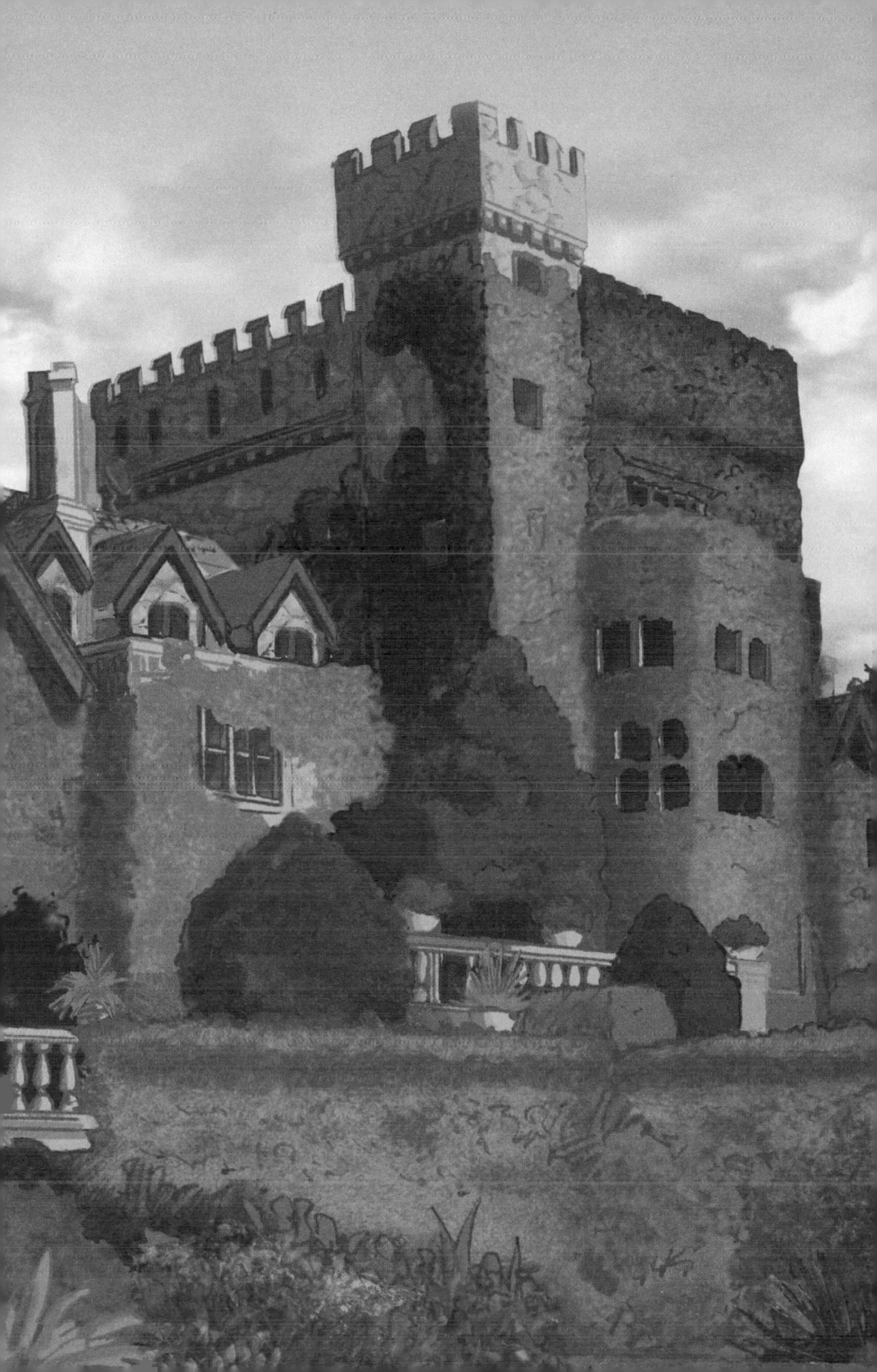

A long time ago, two men started
this school for kids who were
different from everyone else.
How were they different?
They had special powers.

Powers that the people around them—

their parents, other kids—

did not understand.

This is a school for mutants.

Some of the students stayed on at
the school once they were finished.

They became teachers.

They are known as the X-Men.

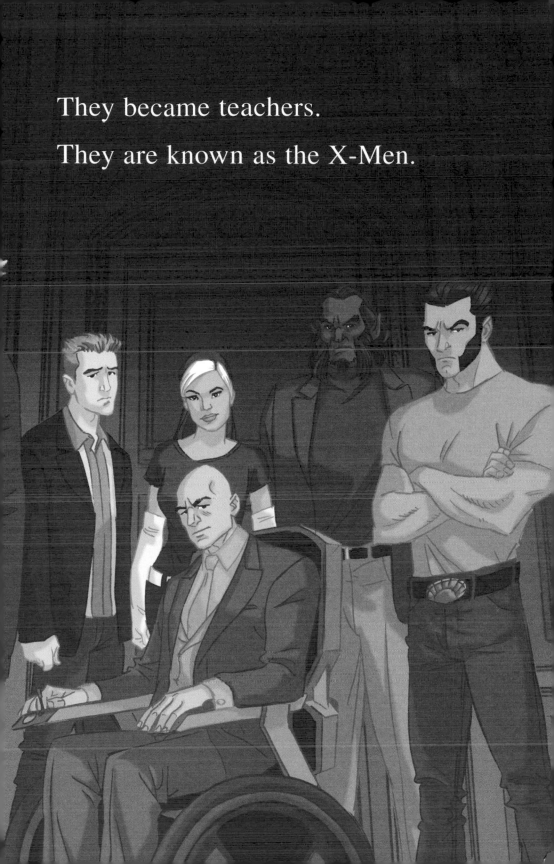

Professor X runs the school.

His psychic powers are very strong.

He can read minds.

He can make people think whatever
he wants—and they never know
he's doing it.

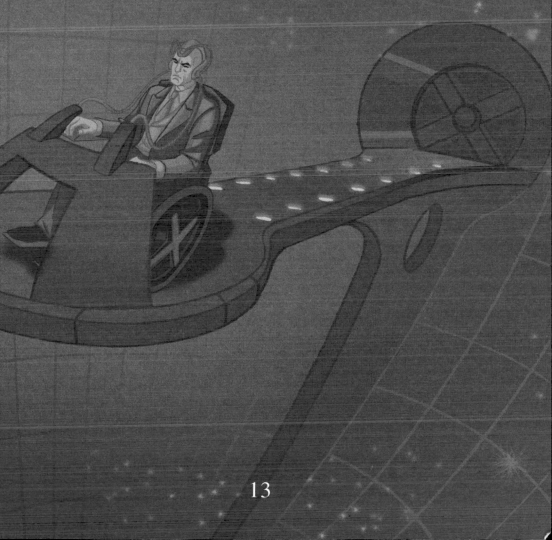

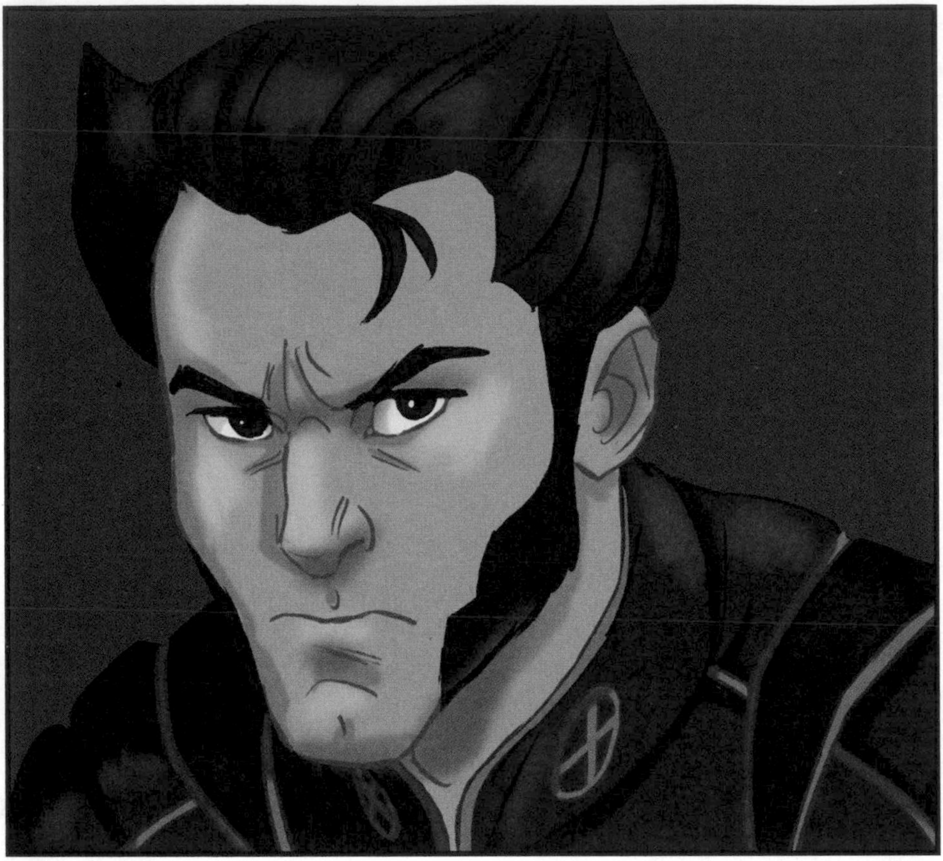

Wolverine is one of the most mysterious mutants.
He has special healing powers.
No matter how badly someone hurts him, his wounds heal in seconds.

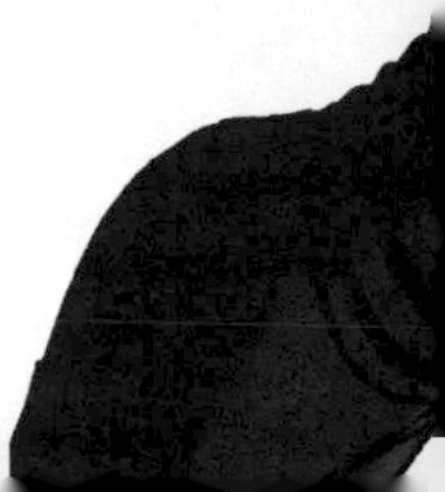

Wolverine has metal claws
attached to his bones.
When he gets angry,
the claws pop out.

Storm has a very special power.

She can control the weather.

She can make it snow or rain,

or even create a tornado.

Storm can control the air so that
she can fly.
You can tell when Storm is using
her powers, because her eyes
start to glow.

Rogue's powers make it hard
for her to be close to people.
If she touches someone, she absorbs
his or her memories, abilities, and
life force.

If Rogue touches a mutant,
she has the mutant's powers
for a few minutes.
But if she touches someone for too long,
she can kill the person.
She has to wear gloves.

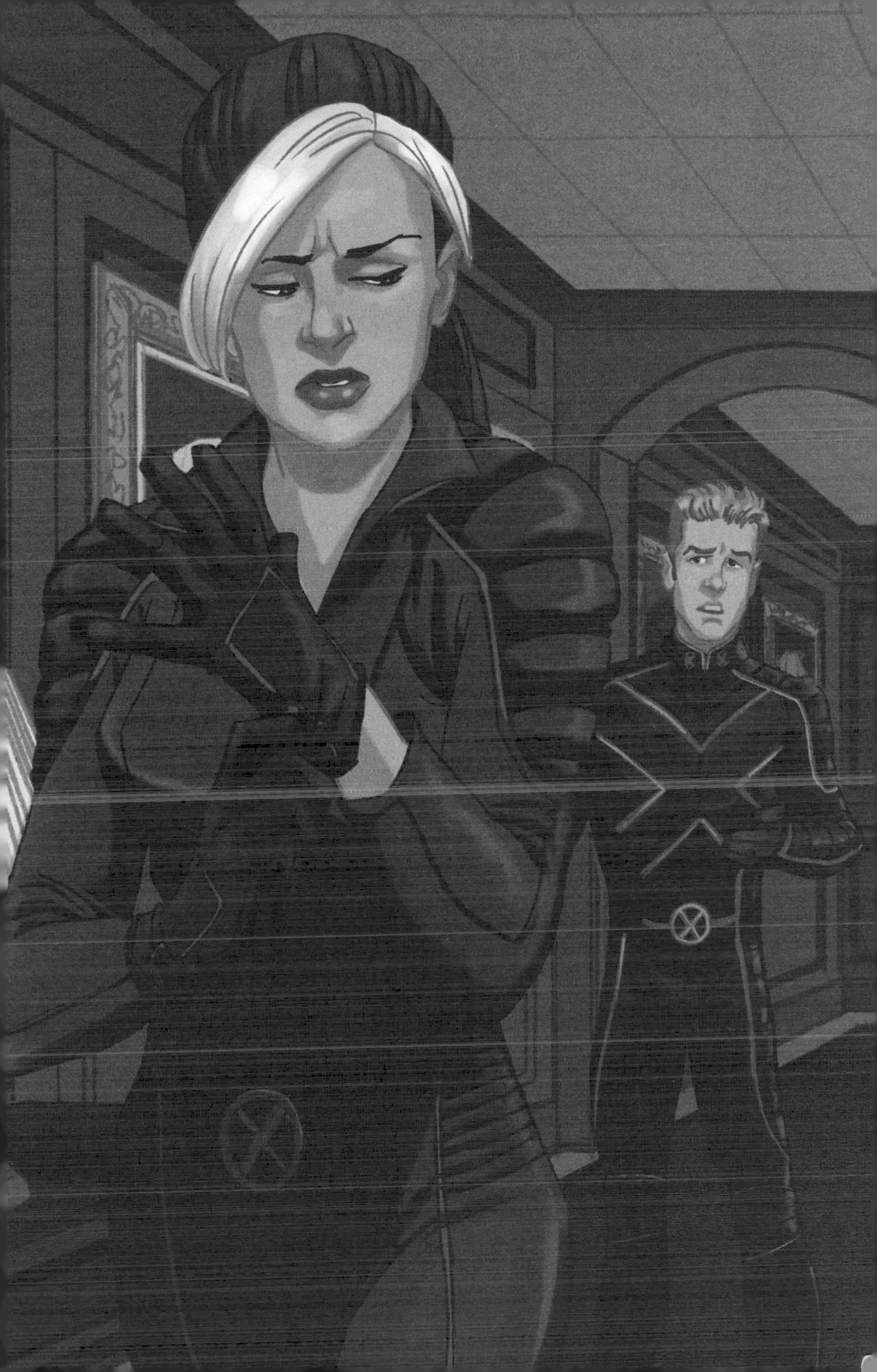

Iceman is Rogue's friend.

He can make it so cold that the air
turns to a solid sheet of ice.

He can shoot a blast of icy air
from his hands.

Iceman can turn anything into an
ice cube.

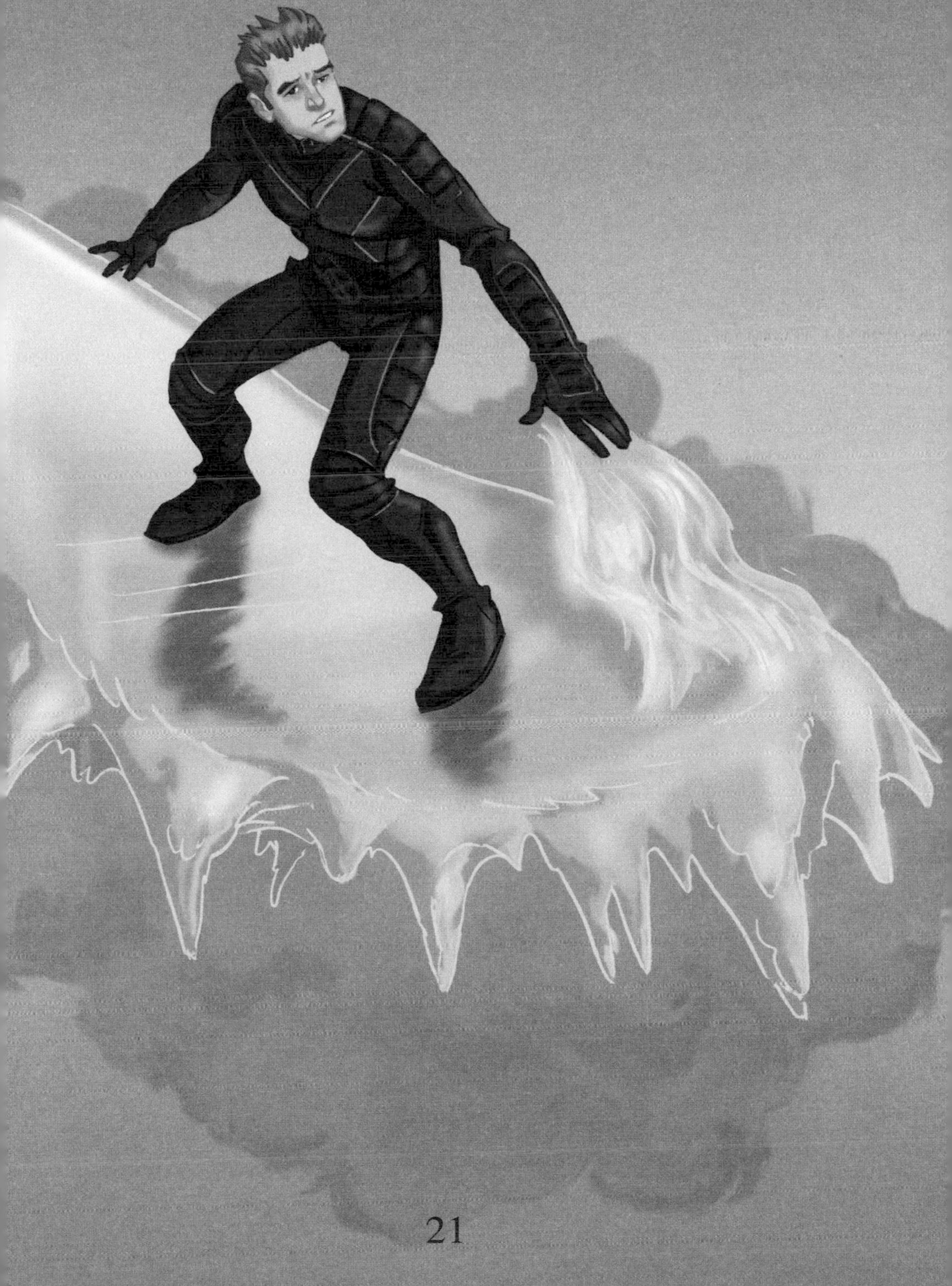

Colossus is strong—very strong.
But when he changes from a human
made of flesh and blood
into a man made of steel, he is
unstoppable.

He can turn to steel—and back again—
in seconds.

Kitty Pryde can pass right through a
solid wall and come out the other side.

She has to move quickly, though.

She cannot breathe when she is

inside something.

Kitty can walk on air, too.

Angel has wings that help him fly.
His wings are so strong that he can
fly while carrying very heavy things.

When Angel needs to hide his wings,
he presses them very close to his body.
They do not show under his clothes.

Beast has superhuman strength.

He is fast.

He never gets tired.

His acrobatic abilities are amazing.

If Beast gets hurt, his wounds heal quickly.

Humans have never understood what it is like to be a mutant. Sometimes they even try to hurt mutants.

But the X-Men always try to do
what is right.

They work together to make the world a
better place for both humans and mutants.
The X-Men have been given
amazing powers.
They must do amazing things.